Sassafras
Goes to Hollywood

By Lynn Hirshfield and Dena Fishbein

PSS!
PRICE STERN SLOAN

For my "It" mother, Pola Hirshfield, whose love is boundless and for my "It" sister Suzi Hirshfield, rescuer of people and pets. To my "It" son Eli whom I adore and for our not so "It" dog Dewey whom we love anyway. I love you all very, very, very much, Lynn

For our spoiled poodle, Ruby, who inspired this book, and most of all to my husband, Danny, who has been the love of my life since high school. — Dena

Thank you to the following "It" colleagues and friends: Bonnie Bader, Merrilee Heifetz, Jesse and Stephen Nathan, Caroline Lister, Ian Corson, Susan Cartsonis, Aline Grunwald, Barbara Perlin, Andy Cohen, Gary Pearl, Margi English, Laura Edwards, Nana Greenwald, Helen Storey, Cheryl Goldstein, Gina Shelton, Honor Moshay, Buffy Shutt, Kathy Jones, Ricky Strauss, Jeff Skoll, Jim Berk, and the rest of the gang at Participant Productions. Sassie's heart and soul belong to the dedicated volunteers of Much Love Animal Rescue. Please consider adopting an animal and supporting this organization by visiting their website www.muchlove.org. XO, Lynn

A great big special thanks to Heidi Van Winkle for being the very, very, very fabulous graphic designer that she is. — Dena

PRICE STERN SLOAN
Published by the Penguin Group
Penguin Group (USA) Inc., 375 Hudson Street, New York, New York 10014, U.S.A.
Penguin Group (Canada), 90 Eglinton Avenue East, Suite 700, Toronto, Ontario, Canada M4P 2Y3 (a division of Pearson Penguin Canada Inc.)
Penguin Books Ltd, 80 Strand, London WC2R 0RL, England
Penguin Ireland, 25 St Stephen's Green, Dublin 2, Ireland (a division of Penguin Books Ltd)
Penguin Group (Australia), 250 Camberwell Road, Camberwell, Victoria 3124, Australia (a division of Pearson Australia Group Pty Ltd)
Penguin Books India Pvt Ltd, 11 Community Centre, Panchsheel Park, New Delhi - 110 017, India
Penguin Group (NZ), 67 Apollo Drive, Mairangi Bay, Auckland 1311, New Zealand (a division of Pearson New Zealand Ltd)
Penguin Books (South Africa) (Pty) Ltd, 24 Sturdee Avenue, Rosebank, Johannesburg 2196, South Africa

Penguin Books Ltd, Registered Offices:
80 Strand, London WC2R 0RL, England

Library of Congress Cataloging-in-Publication Data is available.

ISBN 978-0-8431-2191-9   10 9 8 7 6 5 4 3 2

Hello, my darling fans! Yes, it's me—Sassie the Poodle Princess. The one and only, Her Royal Highness Sassafras. I have big news to share with you. I'm going to be a movie star! Fur real!

HOLLYWOOD

To: My Fans
All over the
WORLD XOX

HOW
TO
BE
A
STAR

Norton, that dear man who rescued me when I was lost on the street, heard about the most marvelous contest with a fabulous prize. Hollywood was looking for the next 'It Dog.' And the winner gets to star in a movie. Norton simply insisted on sending in my photo and, well, of course . . . I won a spot in the finals!

A home for every dog, and a dog for every home

I am a Royal Bedrosian Long-Necked Spotted Poodle. A one of a kind! And Norton is a world-famous dog expert. We live at the Much Love Animal Rescue Center, where my job is to help find new homes for lost or forgotten pets. But if Hollywood wanted me to be their new 'It Dog,' how could I refuse?

"Sassie, let's go. We have a long drive ahead of us," said Norton.

Was it time to go already? I wasn't sure if I'd packed enough outfits.

Oh, but what a silly poodle princess I am! They probably had a whole

closet full of glamorous costumes waiting for me!

"Break a leg, Sassie!" yelled out Buster as we drove away. I know that means "good luck" in showbiz talk.

"Good-bye, my darlings," I called back. "I won't forget you!" And then I howled as loud as I could, "Hollywood, here I come!"

Movie stars have fans. I have royal subjects. Whatever they are called, they both love us. And we both have the Pawparazzi following us wherever we go. You know—those reporters who are always flashing their cameras in front of our faces. The only thing I had to do was practice my autograph.

I wondered what kind of movie I'd be starring in. I'm so talented, I could play just about any part. A beautiful young actress like me is called an "ingénue." That's pronounced *onn-je-nuuuuuuuu*, and you should always draw out the *nuuuuuuuuu* to sound like you know what you're talking about.

No need for a stunt dog with me in the starring role. I'm a born athlete.

Did you think I was actually going to faint?
I'm so good, I made myself cry!

"Danger" is my middle name. Don't I look beautiful in black-and-white?

I'm so perfectly funny!

They love me. They really, really love me!

"It's an honor just to be nominated, but it's so very, very, VERY much better to win!"

"Sassie, rise and shine. We're here," said Norton as he parked the van. I stretched my paws and looked out the window. Suddenly, I felt that coming to Hollywood was a big mistake.

I saw dogs of all sizes, shapes, and colors. Every one of them looked like a movie star. Slinky setters and poofy-maned Pomeranians. The hair on that hound was shining like glass! They were simply dazzling.

And there were people called "stylists" fussing and fluffing and following them about. Not only did these dogs all LOOK like winners, they ACTED like winners, too!

And look at me! My fluffy fur had gone flat. My homemade outfit was completely out of style. What made me think I could ever be the 'It Dog'? I wanted to go home! But then Norton did the dearest thing ever.

"My sweet Sassie, don't be nervous," said Norton. "You don't need to win a contest to prove you are special. You and your big heart are IT for me. Just bark the word, and we'll head on out of this circus."

I took a long look at my heart-shaped tail. It IS pretty unique. No stylist needed here. No pink fur in this crowd, either.

It WAS such a long drive. And this meant so much to my friends at the shelter. And to Norton. I didn't want to let that lovely man down.

Okay, I was ready for my close-up!

"Hold on there, Sassie! We have to wait our turn," Norton said.
There must have been dozens of dogs ahead of me, so I barked.
"They don't expect ME to wait in line, do they? Don't they know
WHO I AM?"

"Welcome, contestants, to the 2007 Hollywood 'It Dog' Contest."
We all turned toward the man standing in the spotlight on the stage.
"I am Nick Slick, the master of ceremonies for the competition. And
serving as this year's canine celebrity judge is the star of the new
hit film *The Dog Barked Twice*... Miss Lana Afghan!"

Lana Afghan? She's my favorite! And she was even more breath-taking in person. We all jumped up to give her a standing ovation. Then Nick called out, "And now for the Parade of the Pooches." That was my cue. I was so excited, I could hardly stand it!

It was almost my turn to go when Norton and I heard an angry voice behind us in line. "You better win this contest, Gracie. Otherwise, I'm through with you," said the trainer to a whimpering greyhound. "And stop whining before the judges hear you!" he scolded. Norton's face turned dark red. I could tell he didn't like what he was hearing. Neither did I.

"Next up is Princess Sassafras," called Nick, "whose special talent is . . ." He searched through his cards. My special talent? They expect me to DO something? I looked around the stage and grabbed every-thing in sight. "She's juggling six dogs! Incredible!" Now if I could just make it to the curtain . . . Oh, no!

CCCCRRRRRAAAAASSSHHHHH! Dogs went flying in every direction. "Sorry, my darlings, but thanks for your help!" I said, although they were a little too dizzy to hear me.

"Sassie, I think you just might win this contest," said Norton. He was more excited than I was!

The audience favorites were me—of course—and Gracie. "You are the fastest greyhound I've ever seen," I told her.

She responded sadly, "Thank you. And your pink fur is really pretty. I'm sure you'll win."

I knew she was right. Who could compete with this tail? But it wasn't fair for me to win. Let's face it: I'm a very, very, very lucky dog. I have Norton. I mean, really—what more could a dog wish for? Then Nick announced the winner: "Our 2007 Hollywood 'It Dog' is . . ."

"FAWNA AFGHAN!" Lana Afghan's niece? How typical

"Gracie, you are such a loser!" screamed the mean trainer. Nobody
talks to dogs that way around Norton. He ordered the trainer out the
door while I held Gracie's paw.

"Who needs Hollywood when we have Much Love, where every dog is
a star? Gracie, you're coming home with us!"

"Sassie, it's this big heart right here that makes you so special."
And with those words he actually made me blush a brighter shade
of pink.

Before we climbed back into the van, I accidentally stepped into wet cement on the sidewalk. Now I've really left my mark on this town—movie-star style!

1. Always sing louder than anyone else in the room, even if you don't know the words.

2. When signing autographs, write in big, curly letters that fill the whole page.

3. The world is your stage. The people in it— your fans.

4. Sunglasses are an absolute must for all wannabe celebrities! Especially indoors.

Extra-credit tip for superstars:

No matter how famous you become, always remember where you came from and don't forget the people who got you there.

Love and Kisses,

Princess Sassie,

HRH The Royal Bedrosian Long-necked Spotted Poodle

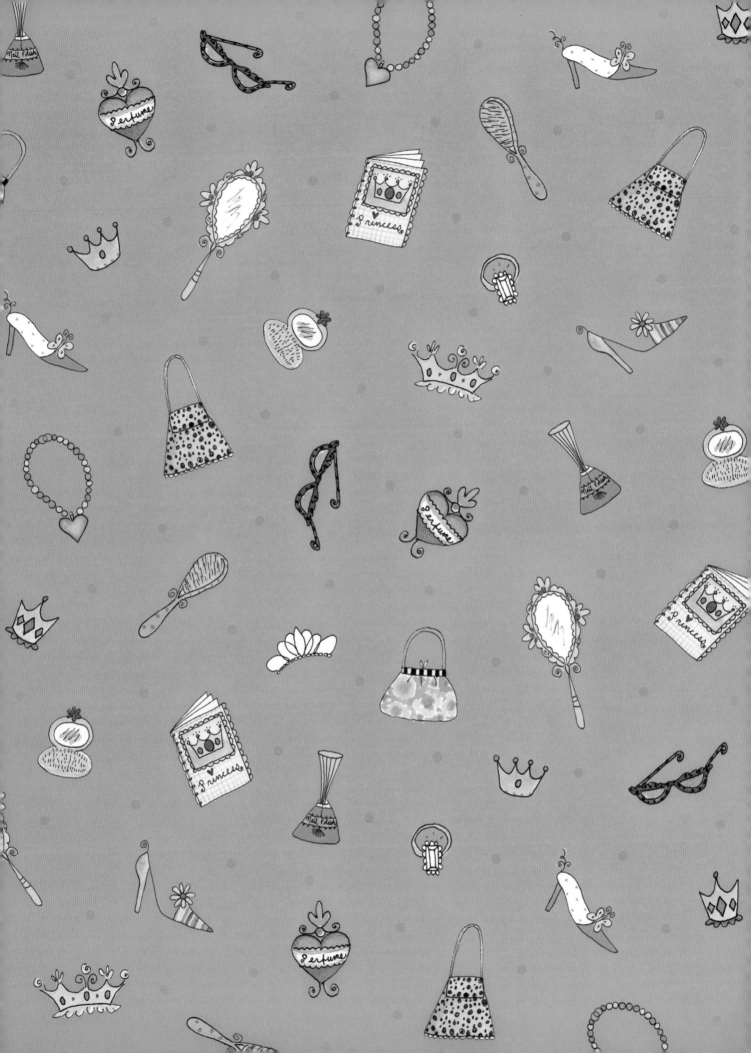

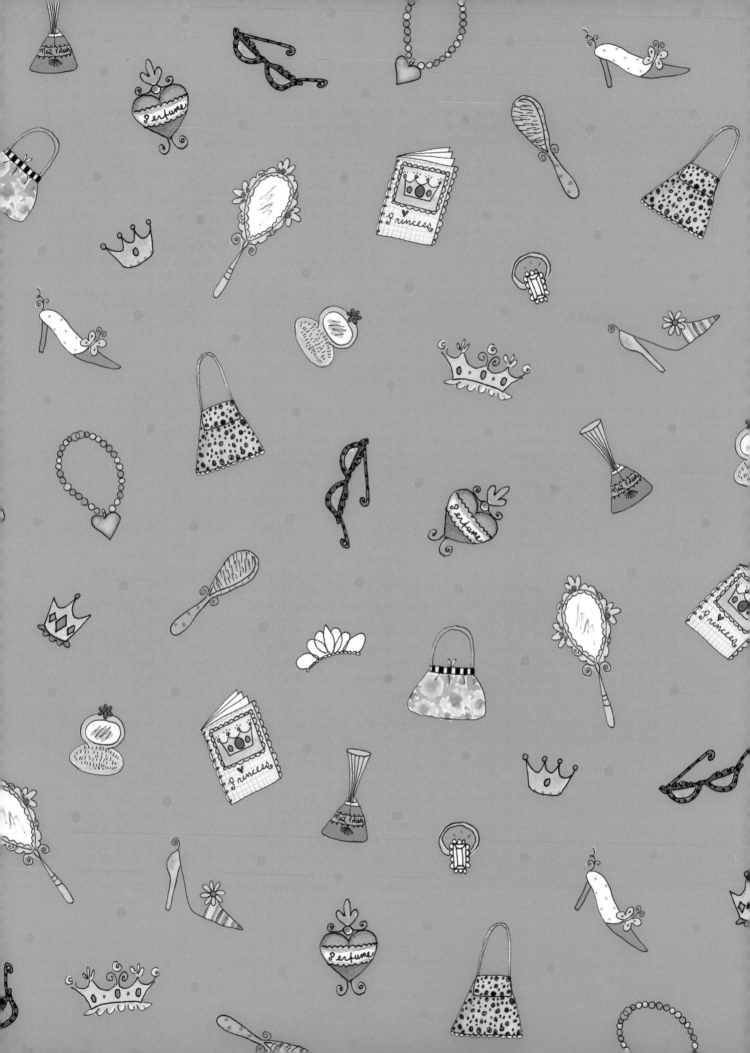